TAMING THEM HARD

Steamy MMF Ménage

Michael Levi

ISBN: 9798832513072
Imprint: Independently published

2nd edition

Cover design by: Michael Levi

CONTENTS

CHAPTER 1

I looked at the question in front of me, my mind trying to make sense of the series of words. Sweat was rolling down my face as the seconds passed by. Professor Derek Azis was pacing from one side of the classroom to the other, trying to make sure nobody would cheat on his test.

By my side was my suitemate. He was a muscular, tall, and confident guy. He looked at me when the professor was far away from us; his eyes were demanding for me to share my answers with him. I shook my head slowly and slightly until he looked back at his test.

Concluding that staying here would not help me find the answer, I stored my stuff back into my backpack, headed to the professor, and handed him my test. He took a good look at it before storing the test in his bag. When I was about to leave the classroom, I looked back and found Damian looking back at me. There was nothing to say or insinuate, so I just left.

I decided to wait for Damian outside of the classroom since the test was about to end soon. He trudged out of the classroom after everyone else minus the professor had left. The blank look on his face was that of someone who knew he had fucked up big time.

"I'm fucked, man!" He exclaimed while we walked to the dining hall.

"Me too", was all I could muster after that very difficult test. It was my first time taking a midterm, so I was worried about my possible lack of success with it.

"You too? Jesus! I thought internationals were supposed to be smart."

"Well, maybe I'm the exception."

"To be honest, since it's your first test here, maybe you just need to adapt. Missing Argentina's university already?"

"Huh? No, of course not. I haven't been here that long yet."

After we sat down to have dinner in the dining hall, one of our mutual friends, a young gal named Jess, sat beside Damian. She was a beautiful brunette with big and plump breasts who had no shame in showing just how happy she was about her body.

"How was the first test of the semester, guys?" She enthusiastically asked while slicing the steak on her plate.

"Bad, terribly bad," Damian replied while he took a sip of his orange juice.

"Same here…", I said while looking down, unable to feel joy at the moment.

"Sounds like Mateo needs to learn a bit how the tests work here", she said.

"Yeah, I think I do. Hopefully, I can make up for that later, though."

Damian put his fork and knife down on the table. His plate was full of food, so I wondered why he did that. When I looked up, his eyes were flashing with purpose.

"I've got a plan", he announced while looking at the ceiling.

"And what would that be, big man?" Jess asked, mocking him.

Damian's eyes still flashed with excitement when he continued, "Why not enter professor Derek's office at night when everyone is sleeping?"

Jess spat out her grape juice over the table as I choked my food. When I stopped coughing, Damian looked at each of us and said once again, "This is no joke, y'all."

"Right", Jess replied, her tone showing that she wasn't taking him seriously.

"There's no way that can work. We would most likely be caught", I rebuked while cleaning my mouth with a napkin.

"There's something about me you don't know yet", he said, his eyes flashing brighter once more.

"And what would that be?" Jess asked, now genuinely curious.

"I've got a friend who works with the security team. He can disable the cameras and the electronic locks."

Jess spat out her drink again and I used another napkin to clean up the table.

"Just don't get me involved", Jess said while she prepared to leave. Damian grabbed her arm and forced her to sit down. "Hey!" She protested, but Damian was stubborn.

"You're going to be on guard duty. You will stay outside to make sure nobody comes and finds us."

"No way!"

"I'll pay you."

Jess squinted her eyes and asked, "How much?"

"As much as you want."

Jess narrowed her eyes even further, and then she looked at me. I shrugged.

"Fine, I will be your guard. But you will have to pay as much as I want", she said while getting up from the chair.

"Send me a message with more details", she continued before heading out of the dining hall.

"You are coming as well, Mateo", Damian said after we both finished having dinner. Given that I didn't want to start college on the wrong foot, I accepted his proposal.

CHAPTER 2

It was the day after that talk we had in the dining hall when Damian announced his plan to save our grades. He had sent Jess messages containing the information she needed. She still didn't look completely comfortable helping us, but I knew she was reliable.

Damian was sitting on the couch when I stepped out of the bathroom. He took a good look at my lean body before frowning.

"You should at least hit the gym a couple of times a week, dude", he said while typing on his phone.

I looked down, trying to find something wrong with my body. I had always been skinny like that my whole life, and being the bottom that I was, it fitted me.

I shrugged and responded, "No way. I like the way I am. You spend more time at the gym than studying, so maybe you are the one who should have your priorities rechecked."

Damian opened up a wicked smile after that provocation from me. He grabbed a pillow from the couch and threw it at me. I evaded it easily as it hit the wall behind me.

The jock wore just his boxer briefs. His bulge was looking plump and meaty. My mouth was salivating with desire.

"At least take that towel off so that I can have a better look at you", he demanded while grabbing his bulge and vulgarly teasing it for me.

Staring at his bulge, and unable to move my body, I slowly let the towel fall to the floor. The cold air of the room made me feel goosebumps all over my body. Damian sized me up before his eyes stopped at my swelling cockette.

He spread his hairy, thick legs further apart, which made his bulge look even bigger than before. Naked as when I was born, I crept over to him. My eyes were still staring at his oversized and plump bulge.

"You know what to do, babe", he said while caressing my hair. I found out he was bisexual during my second day living in this residence hall when he was licking the pussy of a fellow student. His response to me showing up out of nowhere was to let me suck his big man tool alongside his former girlfriend, which I gladly accepted.

With my hands trembling, I slowly slid down his boxer briefs. Given how muscular and huge he was, even a size G was too small for him. His cock sprung out looking very assured and ready to be serviced. It was not fully hard yet and was resting on his leg, waiting for my next move.

I slowly reached over with my small hand, trying to envelop his member with my little fingers. Damian's huge hand moved away from my head when he rested his head on the couch, looking very much on the verge of waiting to have the best blowjob of his life. When I squeezed his big man tool, he emitted a long moan of pleasure that reverberated in the living room.

Afraid of doing this too quickly, I stroked him up and down slowly. His cock began to grow harder quickly, opening my hand. My hand was barely enough to cover about half of his circumference when he was fully hard.

His musky scent was almost intoxicating. My lungs were being filled and penetrated by his scent. I inhaled as much of it as I could before wrapping my lips around the glands of his oversized shaft.

Damian rested his hand on my head once again, forcing me to go down even more on his member. Once I had a couple more inches inside me, I struggled against the strength of his hand. He noticed my hesitation to go further down, and being the generous man he was, he changed his mind.

As I bobbed up and down on him, I also played with his scrotum. Even with the cold air of the AC, the air was still warm. I kept on sucking his member, worshiping the much bigger man while I fumbled and played with his testicles.

As time passed, I finally felt Damian on the verge of releasing his load inside my hungry mouth. Since I didn't want to swallow him then, I slid my mouth off his member and waited for Damian to aim it at me.

As I stepped away from him, still on my knees, Damian got up from the couch instantly and aimed his big shaft at me. I saw it twitch one last time before the first rope of jism hit my upper lip.

Damian shot more and more ropes of pure joy all over my face. "I haven't cummed all week", he said with difficulty while he tried to catch his breath after each jet of cum. Those words only served to increase my libido, making my small cock shoot out sperm all over the carpet.

My face was sticky and fully covered with his seeds when I used my towel to clean myself up. As I got up from the floor, Damian squeezed my butt with his masculine hand before padding over to the bathroom.

As he closed the door and I sat down on the exact spot he was sitting on the couch, I realized just how lucky I was, having him for a suitemate.

CHAPTER 3

Damian slowly used the key to open the door for Jess and me, and it led to a hallway. As he held it open, we walked in.

Damian, Jess, and I headed to the end of the hallway, where the office was located. My suitemate had the keys for it as well, so with the cameras and security locks turned off, he slowly opened the door.

The office was familiar to me. The blue light of the moon highlighted the desk where the computer was, while also hiding the large pot plants the professor had.

"We've got this. Jess, stay outside", Damian ordered.

"On it", she said before closing the door.

Derek started to rifle through the drawers in professor Derek's desk. Meanwhile, I searched the drawers in the cabinets on the walls.

Minutes later, when I was on the other side of the office, I finally found what seemed to be the folder containing the next test.

"Derek, I've found it", I said with enthusiasm while I handed him the folder. He opened it and looked at the test in front of him.

He grabbed the sheet of paper and smiled. "We can study for his next test now. We will get an A+ this time!" He said before sliding back the open drawers.

He gave me the folder, which I put back into the drawer where I found it.

"Let's head out. Jess probably wants to kill us right now after we dragged her into this," I said while heading to the door.

Just when I was about to place my hand on the doorknob, Jess hurriedly opened it and stepped back into the office. Her eyes and mouth were wide open; she looked as if she'd just seen a ghost.

Worried, I asked while she closed the door using Damian's key, "What happened?"

"It's Mr. Will. He is coming down this hallway! Let's stay quiet until he passes by here."

Damian, Jess, and I sat on the floor, with our backs against the wall as we heard Mr. Will whistling gently. It sounded closer and closer as the seconds passed by.

He stopped in front of the office, and I heard his hand trying to open the door. I covered Jess's mouth with my hand so that she didn't give us away.

"Shhhhhh!"

The doorknob was still shaking.

"Strange, I thought I saw someone entering," Mr. Will remarked.

He tried the doorknob again and again. My head was pounding, my heart was racing and sweat was rolling down my face. I looked to the sides, where Jess and Damian were, and found they were as frightened as I was.

I closed my eyes while I prayed for Mr. Will to go away. When the doorknob finally stopped shaking, I still kept them closed, as did Damian and Jess.

"I think he's gone," Jess said before getting up. Still afraid of Mr. Will, I slowly opened my eyes. The blue light from the moon seemed brighter than before.

"Yeah, he really is", Damian confirmed while checking through the doorknob hole.

"Nobody's around, then! Let's get out before someone else comes", Jess said while striding to the door.

She placed her hand on the knob and tried to open it.

"Silly me", she said while opening a smile, "Of course it's closed."

She grabbed the key from her pocket and used it in the keyhole. There was a click, but when she tried to open the door, it remained stuck.

"What's going on, Jess?" Damian asked while grabbing the key from her and trying to force the door open. His muscles flexed and rippled as he tried to unlock it.

"What in the world…?!" He asked himself while trying to open the door again, this time with more force than before. My heart was pounding faster and harder than before as the fear of being stuck here popped up.

Damian collapsed on the floor after he tried to open it one last time. Jess's eyes screamed with worry as she paced from one side of the office to the other. Meanwhile, I stood between them, not knowing what to do.

"Did… Mr. Will just lock us in here?" I asked, not knowing how likely that was.

Jess stopped in her tracks, her eyes flashing with confusion, "That doesn't make sense, Mateo! None of this does! I closed the door, so how the hell did he close it a second time?!"

"You are right, Jess…", I said while looking down. I sat on the floor and rested my back and head on the wall.

"What are we going to do now?" I asked while Damian remained on the floor, his hands covering his face.

"I don't know, man. If professor Derek finds us here, we're screwed! We'll certainly get kicked out."

Shock crossed my face, facing the realization of losing my scholarship and coming back home without finishing my exchange program.

As I looked outside, I spotted a snowflake hitting and melting against the glass of the window. Curious to find out about what was happening, I stepped over there.

Jess glanced at me with curious eyes when she saw me passing by her. I placed my hands on the window and looked up. More and more snowflakes were falling from the sky. In a matter of seconds, there was a layer of snow all over the garden behind the office.

Damian stepped to the window and stood beside me.

"Strange", he started to say, "It's not supposed to snow at this time of the year."

CHAPTER 4

Ice and snow were the only things I could see when looking out the window. Ever since it started snowing, I didn't notice a single moment when it wasn't. It was turning into a raging blizzard, and we couldn't do anything about it.

"What are we going to do now? It's been ten days already. If it weren't for the food and water professor Derek had stored here, we would be dead already!" I said, each word showing just how frustrated I was.

"I don't know, Mateo, but I'm scared", Jess said while her eyes got teary.

Damian, who was looking at his phone screen, said, "Nothing on when the blizzard will stop. The authorities have no idea what's the cause of it."

"Fuck!" I said while I kicked professor Derek's desk.

"It's not all bad. Wanna know what's on my mind right now, Mateo?" Damian asked, his eyes flashing with lust.

"We don't have the time for that, Damian", I grumbled, each word expressing how frustrated I was.

"But... this is the perfect time, don't you see? We are stuck here, just the two of us and Jess. Plus, it's the professor's office. How many times did you do it in a place like this?"

Just as those words came out of his mouth, I felt my cock getting harder and my asshole contracting with pleasure.

I looked up at him, and our eyes locked. He slowly enveloped his arm around my shoulder, pulling me closer to him. I rested my head on his waist, offering it to him. He placed his hand on me and started to massage my hair. I closed my eyes, allowing him to bring me immense pleasure.

"You guys… are not seriously going to have sex here, right?" Jess asked, shock crossing her eyes.

"Don't you wanna join us?" I asked, my eyes still closed while Damian continued to massage my head.

"You know…", she started to say before dragging herself close to us, "I think I would like that, too."

Damian opened up a wicked smile before kissing his friend. Before then, I knew they had never even gotten close to doing such a thing. Having seen her predisposition to play with us, I opened my eyes in surprise.

"Just this time, okay?" She asked while rubbing my hair and poking at my cheek.

Her lips connected to mine while Damian played with her plump boobs. I felt my cock stiffening, trying as much as it could to achieve freedom. I hurriedly slid down my pants and briefs and exposed my member to the cold air around us.

The air in the room was getting warmer as the seconds passed. Jess slowly took off Damian's white t-shirt, exposing his strong torso to my cheeks. I gracefully licked his round pecs before I played with his big nipples. Damian moaned in pleasure when I squeezed them with my lips.

Then, Jess took off her shirt and skirt. Her big and generous breasts hung free in front of her, asking to be indulged by my mouth. I slowly wrapped my lips around one of her nipples, which made her moan in pleasure.

I took advantage of the situation to slide down Damian's jeans. I threw them to the other side of the office, where they fell on top of Jess's garments. With a swift movement, Damian took off my shirt and sniffed my armpit.

"That scent… It's SOOOO good!", He energetically said before chucking the shirt away as well. Then, as Jess kissed Damian, their lips rubbing and making noises of pleasure, I took off her bra and panties.

I smelled the two of them for a couple of seconds until the scent infected every cell of my lungs. Looking a bit irritated, Damian picked up my underwear and sniffed it too. Looking at him, I felt waves of pleasure building up as he cherished my smell again.

"Oh, Damian...", Jess chuckled before connecting her lips with his once again. I felt Damian's long and thick member growing under me, begging to be released right away. I didn't like seeing his prick jailed in his pants, and thus I thrust them down without showing a hint of shame.

I sniffed his underwear for a couple of seconds, allowing my lungs to be filled with immense pleasure once again. His musky scent was as masculine and intense as ever.

Jess snatched my underwear before taking a long sniff as well. I noticed the same expression on her face as when Damian smelled her bra and panties.

Instead of tossing the briefs away, she put them between her breasts, offering Damian to get creative. He collected it with his teeth and then landed his lips on hers, letting her moan passionately.

Rather than being an obstacle, the briefs were working as some sort of libido enhancer. Their passionate kiss felt intenser, longer, and tender. I looked at the two of them with envy for not being part of the action.

Noticing the annoyance in my eyes, Damian lowered his head. I contemplated his thick and pink lips slowly floating down while the aroma of his mint toothpaste filled my lungs.

When his lips finally connected with mine, I felt as if I was in heaven. My whole body was trembling with pleasure as his tongue danced and played with my mouth. His lips were big and soft, and they melted my whole heart in an instant.

His huge member was begging to be serviced, so I got up and offered my hand to Jess, which she took. Damian rose and started to walk over to professor Derek's fancy leather chair.

As he sat on the chair, Jess and I hurried to kneel in front of him. His huge scrotum hung low and his cock stood proud. Some pre-cum was seeping out of his slit, and he was inviting us to get a little taste of it.

Jess was the first one to go, gobbling and slurping on his big man tool. Since I didn't want to lag behind, I cupped his balls and started to suck on each of them. I spent a couple of seconds on each before moving to the other. Damian, in the meantime, was rubbing and massaging our heads while speaking words of approval.

"C'mon, you two. That's it! Oh my goodness!"

I finally ran along the length of his shaft with my small tongue, stopping where Jess was playing. She was still dominating his big cockhead, while her saliva made his skin shimmer under the gentle light coming from the outside.

Jess gave his cock a couple of kisses before allowing me to play with his gland. We changed positions so that she could play with his heavy testicles. Before I had even touched his head with my soft lips, she was already all over the balls of the big muscular man.

I closed my eyes and took a deep breath before lunging forward. My lips wrapped around the glans of the athletic man, making me feel even more aroused. Damian emitted another long groan when my tongue started to play with his silky-smooth skin.

"I know you're loving this, but wanna do something else and change things up a bit?" He asked after we spent minutes savoring his dick.

Jess and I furrowed our brows. Noticing our reaction, Damian explained, "I'm not about to stop this now if that's what you're concerned about."

Jess turned around on her knees, her glistening pussy now facing Damian's big, manly cock. The athletic man opened up a wide, wicked smile before getting on his knees. He was now straddling her while his dick tried to cave a way in.

Since I didn't want to be left out, I scooted under Jess and planted my hands on her breasts. She closed her eyes while I fumbled with them. They were so plump and huge that I couldn't help but suck on each of them. Her hard nipples were of special delight to me.

Jess's body was now moving forward and backward while Damian thrust in and out of her. I couldn't believe they were fucking, unprotected, in the professor's office. This couldn't get any wilder.

None of them seemed to care that they had crossed boundaries nobody should have. Both still had their eyes closed while clinging to whatever they could for support. Jess's hands were on my waist, digging into my skin, while Damian's huge, masculine hand carved the woman's buttcheeks.

I just stood there sucking and playing with her nipples and breasts while Damian kept on ramming in and out of her moist cunt. Looking down where his cock met her pussy, I could see their muscles and skin tightening in response to the exerted efforts.

I reached forward with my tiny little fingers to cup his balls once again. They were so hot that my hand almost got burned. I quickly withdrew it from there before trying again. Once I was accustomed to the temperature, I played with his balls one more time.

"You two have no idea how much I'm loving this," Damian purred, his eyes now open and looking lucid.

"What are you saying?" Jess asked, fighting for breathing. Even I was finding breathing difficult right now.

"I mean, I've always wanted to do the two of you. I just never thought that it would happen here."

"You know", I began to say while moving to the side so that I could look Damian in his eyes, "I never thought Jess was going to change her mind about this so suddenly."

"Shut up, you two", she said while slapping the two of us in the face. I felt my right cheek stinging.

"Ouch, that hurt!", Damian said before thrusting into the woman another time.

"Let's just not pause again, okay?" She pleaded before kissing me on the lips. She planted her hands on Damian's ass and forced him to put more inches inside of her.

"I'm just so close to having the orgasm of my life right now", she huffed while licking her own lips.

"I know," Damian purred before opening his smile again and thrusting her pussy harder. Her pussy juices were dripping out, and I couldn't help myself. I had to lick them, and it was like being in heaven.

"It's coming!" she shouted before her body began to tremble in pleasure.

"Shit! I've got to hold you tight right now, babe," Damian announced while his own body started to shake as well.

His cock stiffened at the same time her vulva shut close around it. The two had their orgasms at the same time. Their mixed substances were rolling down their combined bodies, which I also swallowed.

Damian thrust her again, pouring out more of his cum inside of her. I wondered if she was or wasn't ovulating, but then the thought quickly dissipated when another huge load of cum fell into my gaping mouth.

"You two are the best", I said while Damian withdrew his cock from her vulva. A huge glob of cum came out of her slit, filling me up even more.

"Hmmmm! This is so tasty", I cooed while getting up from the floor.

Damian headed to the window and placed his hands on it. I walked up to him and squeezed his butt. He looked at me with a huge smile on his face.

"At least we have each other here," I said. He embraced my shoulders with his huge, masculine arm, forcing me to lay my head on his chest once again.

"Indeed", he murmured into my right ear.

CHAPTER 5

"**R**eady to get an A+ this time?", Damian asked while winking at me.

"Of course! I'm always ready. I'm going to fucking ace it," I enthused before stepping inside the classroom. Damian sat beside me as usual. Once again, I couldn't refrain from contemplating and admiring his huge, athletic arms and legs.

The test started, and just as we suspected, it was exactly like the one we got from professor Derek's office. I answered each question with pure confidence, after having studied them carefully before.

An hour later, after procrastinating a bit so that nobody suspected anything, I handed the paper over to the Professor.

Damian hurried to catch up to me, and he had a huge smile on his face. He patted me on the back as I opened the double doors that led to the exterior.

"How was it?", I winked.

"I could ask you the same", he responded before we burst out laughing.

A week later, the professor finally returned our tests. Damian showed me his, an A+ featuring proudly on the right corner of his paper. I showed mine to him, which also sported the same rating.

Damian patted me on the back before the professor started his lecture. From that point on, I swore I would do much better on the next tests since I didn't plan on cheating again.

Still, considering how easy it was to game the system without any repercussions, maybe it was not such a bad idea. The only problem was: would Jess join us again?

"Think Jess's gonna come looking for more of what we did, Damian?" I asked him while we sat in the dining hall to have lunch.

He chinned up and said, "No reason not to. I know what she's like."

The problem was, though, that ever since the snow melted and we managed to leave the office, none of us managed to find Jess on campus again. Her phone was always offline, which was odd.

But then someone, out of nowhere, patted me on the back when I was about to bite my burger. Looking back to see who it was, I found no other than Jess herself! *Speak of the devil, huh.*

"JESS!" I shouted, which rewarded me with some looks of disapproval from the other students in the dining hall.

She sat beside Damian. My best friend had a wide smile on his face.

After she put her plate on the table, she said, "Long time no see, huh?"

"Yeah, what happened? I tried reaching out, but you never even replied to my messages."

"My dad was worried there was going to be another blizzard, so he dragged me back home. It took me a while to convince him that he was just being paranoid about it. That's why I vanished."

"You know", Damian began to say while taking a bite from his burger, "I would love another blizzard."

We burst out laughing in unison, rewarding ourselves with more looks of disapproval from the other students.

The End

Leave a review if you liked this story. Your feedback helps me improve immensely!

TEASER: SHARING THE ALPHA

Steamy MMF Ménage

"This is going to rock!" Diego, a Chilean friend of mine, said from the passenger seat beside me. It was his first time going to an event outside of the city. He looked at the map once again and stared for a couple of seconds at a spot on the lower left side.

"Only about one thousand people live there?" He asked with an inquisitive face. I looked at his map, then at him before answering, "Yes, Diego. It's a small town, after all."

"I can't wait to go to that Halloween festival. Everyone at college talked a lot about it. I've got so much hype for it that I can barely control myself right now!"

I was as excited to be there as well, but since it was my nth time after many, I wasn't as jubilant as he was. "Yeah. I can't wait to meet the gals there too."

"Sucks that I won't be able to drink anything there because I'm not twenty-one yet. At least you can buy some drinks for me, right?"

"*Right?* And I guess I can go to jail by helping you out, too."

Diego shook his arms about in protest. "But, nobody has to

know anything about it!"

I looked at him with narrowed eyes. "Right. It only takes one good cop to put me in jail."

"Oh! C'mon!"

"Stop it, Diego. Just enjoy your time there. The alcohol won't matter much when the girls are all over you. People there love meeting foreigners."

Diego folded his arms and sighed. "Fine, guess it'll have to do."

The boulevard in front of us was full of cars, and all were seemingly heading in the same direction. Then, the cars slowed down to a crawl before we took a turn to the right. The venue of the event was almost glowing in the distance.

As we approached it, we caught sight of a couple of police cars patrolling the area. We were clean, but I was still worried. I'd heard too often of overzealous cops stopping people from going to Halloween Forever. Diego being with us didn't help as well.

Diego didn't look as worried though, and maybe it was because he was from a completely different country.

As we approached the main gate, one of the police officers asked me to stop. I rolled down the side window and showed him my driving license. He checked it a couple of times before nodding and giving it back. Diego gave the chubby man his passport. The cop scanned the document with his eyes before giving it back.

"All good", he said. I stepped into the pedal to accelerate my sedan until we found a good parking spot. As I pulled up the car between two large SUVs, Diego reached for his backpack to stow his passport.

"What are you doing, man? They might ask for your passport even when you are there."

"Don't care. I just want to have a good time now."

I rolled my eyes. "Fine. It's your funeral if they find you without it."

Diego and I, then, left the sedan. We headed toward the entrance, where a long line was forming. Close to the gate was a dispensary with fliers and other documents which explained a bit about the area...

SIMILAR BOOKS

SERIES - BICURIOUS GUYS

Love in the dorm, professors crossing lines, jocks swinging the other way, and more. This series is all about college steam.

1. Caught Looking by the Quarterback
2. Caught Looking by the Basketeer
3. Caught Looking by the Dropout
4. Caught Looking by the Jock
5. Caught Looking by the Roommate

SERIES - GAY FOR BLUE COLLARS

They are massive, thick, and their hands are extra calloused. These blue collars know no boundaries.

1. Given to the Cop
2. Given to the Miner
3. Given to the Plumber
4. Given to the Firefighter
5. Given to the Mechanic

ABOUT THE AUTHOR

Steamy MM stories, baby! Michael Levi can't go a day without sitting down and putting into words all the dirty scenes that sprout in his mind. His collection is diverse, but it's gay love only. And if you are looking for something free, check his mailing list. Warning: it can be extra spicy.

When Michael Levi isn't writing, he's chilling out by the lake close to his house. Nothing better than kicking back with a martini in his hand as he daydreams his next explicit scenes.